MR. STR

and the flood

Original concept by Roger Hargreaves
Illustrated and written by Adam Hargreaves

MR. MEN LITTLE MISS

World International

Mr Strong is unbelievably strong.

So strong that sometimes he forgets his own strength.

Like the other day.

It was raining.

So Mr Strong pulled on his wellington boots. But he pulled too hard and his foot went right through the bottom of his boot!

Then he went out through his front door and opened his umbrella.

But he pushed too hard and turned the umbrella inside out!

So he tried to go back inside to get another umbrella (Mr Strong gets through a lot of umbrellas) but when he turned the doorknob it came off in his hand.

Poor Mr Strong was not having a good day.

Fortunately, when you are as strong as Mr Strong you don't need a door to get inside your house.

Do you know what he did?

He picked up the corner of his house and slipped in under the wall!

Once he had fetched a new umbrella and opened it (very carefully this time) and opened his door (very carefully) he set off for his walk.

Now as you might remember I mentioned that it was raining.

What I did not tell you was that it had been raining for days and days and days.

Nearly a whole week.

Non-stop!

The river in the valley below Mr Strong's house had burst its banks and was flooding the meadows.

Mr Strong walked down the lane beneath the dripping trees.

It was not long before he met a very worried looking Farmer Fields.

"Good morning," said Mr Strong. "What's the matter?"

"It's my sheep," said Farmer Fields. "They're stuck in the meadow surrounded by water. I can't get them out!"

"Let's go and see," said Mr Strong. "I might be able to help."

Poor Farmer Fields' sheep were indeed in trouble.

And the bit of dry land left for them to stand on was getting smaller by the minute as the flood water rose higher.

Mr Strong waded out to the little island in the middle of the meadow and then waded back carrying two sheep above his head.

"Oh, well done," said Farmer Fields. "The only problem is that there are ninety-eight sheep left out there and we'll run out of time before you've carried them all across!"

"Mmmm," said Mr Strong. "I fear you may be right, but I think I have an idea. Do you mind if I borrow your barn?"

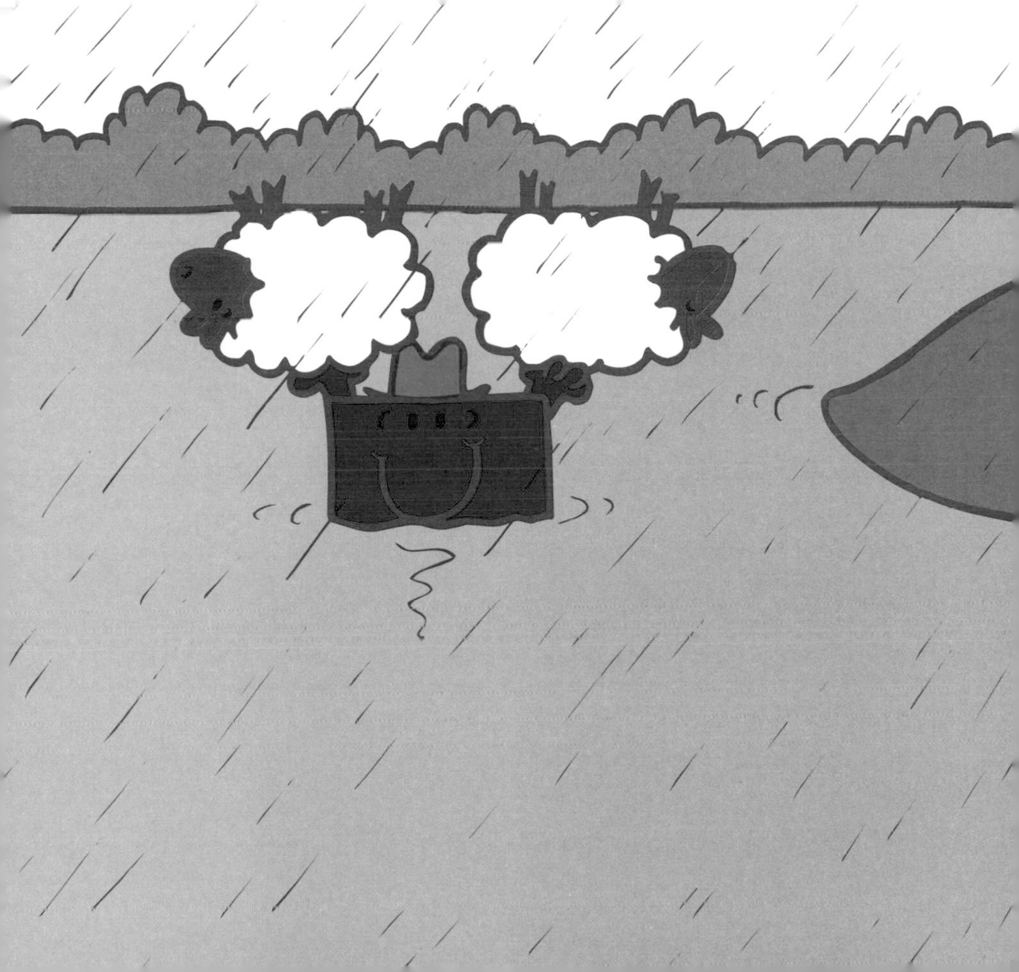

Farmer Fields smiled.

And you are probably smiling if you have read the other story about Mr Strong.

But for those of you who have not read that Mr Strong story, I'll tell you what he did.

He picked up the barn (that's right, a whole barn!) and carried it across to the sheep.

Then he lifted all the sheep into the barn, counting them carefully as he did, so as not to leave any behind.

And then he picked up the barn with all ninety-eight sheep inside, and waded back to Farmer Fields.

"Oh, thank you," said Farmer Fields, once all his sheep were safely in the field at the top of the hill.

"Barns are very handy things to have lying around," chuckled Mr Strong, and went home.

That evening Mr Strong ate an enormous plateful of fried eggs and went to bed early ...

... and fell fast ASHEEP! HA! HA!

•RETURN THIS WHOLE PAGE•

3 Great Offers For Mr Men Fans

1 Token EGMONT WORLD

1 FREE Door Hangers and Posters

In every Mr Men and Little Miss Book like this one you will find a special token. Collect 6 and we will send you either a brilliant Mr. Men or Little Miss poster and a Mr Men or Little Miss double sided, full colour, bedroom door hanger. Apply using the coupon overleaf, enclosing six tokens and a 50p coin for your choice of two items.

Egmont World tokens can be used towards any other Egmont World / World International token scheme promotions., in early learning and story / activity books.

Posters: Tick your preferred choice of either Mr Men ☐ or Little Miss ☐

Door Hangers: Choose from: Mr. Nosey & Mr Muddle ☐, Mr Greedy & Mr Lazy ☐, Mr Tickle & Mr Grumpy ☐, Mr Slow & Mr Busy ☐, Mr Messy & Mr Quiet ☐, Mr Perfect & Mr Forgetful ☐, Little Miss Fun & Little Miss Late ☐, Little MIss Helpful & Little Miss Tidy ☐, Little Miss Busy & Little Miss Brainy ☐, Little Miss Star & Little Miss Fun ☐.
(Please tick)

2 Mr Men Library Boxes

Keep your growing collection of Mr Men and Little Miss books in these superb library boxes. With an integral carrying handle and stay-closed fastener, these full colour, plastic boxes are fantastic. They are just £5.49 each including postage. Order overleaf.

3 Join The Club

To join the fantastic Mr Men & Little Miss Club, check out the page overleaf NOW!

Allow 28 days for delivery. We reserve the right to change the terms of this offer at any time but we offer a 14 day money back guarantee. The money-back guarantee does not affect your statutory rights. Birthday and Christmas cards are sent care of parent/guardians in advance of the day. After 31/12/00 please call to check that the offer details are still correct.

•RETURN THIS WHOLE PAGE•

Join Our Club!

MR. MEN & Little Miss CLUB

When you become a member of the fantastic Mr Men and Little Miss Club you'll receive a personal letter from Mr Happy and Little Miss Giggles, a club badge with your name, and a superb Welcome Pack (pictured below right).

You'll also get birthday and Christmas cards from the Mr Men and Little Misses, 2 newsletters crammed with special offers, privileges and news, and a copy of the 12 page Mr Men catalogue which includes great party ideas.

If it were on sale in the shops, the Welcome Pack alone might cost around £13. But a year's membership is just £9.99 (plus 73p postage) with a 14 day money-back guarantee if you are not delighted!

HOW TO APPLY To apply for any of these three great offers, ask an adult to complete the coupon below and send it with appropriate payment and tokens (where required) to: Mr Men Offers, PO Box 7, Manchester M19 2HD. Credit card orders for Club membership ONLY by telephone, please call: 01403 242727.

To be completed by an adult

❑ **1.** Please send a poster and door hanger as selected overleaf. I enclose six tokens and a 50p coin for post (coin not required if you are also taking up 2. or 3. below).

❑ **2.** Please send ___ Mr Men Library case(s) and ___ Little Miss Library case(s) at £5.49 each.

❑ **3.** Please enrol the following in the Mr Men & Little Miss Club at £10.72 (inc postage)

Fan's Name:______________________ Fan's Address:______________________________

____

______________________________ Post Code:__________________ Date of birth:___/___/___

Your Name:______________________ Your Address:______________________________

____

Post Code:____________ Name of parent or guardian (if not you):______________________

Total amount due: £________ (£5.49 per Library Case, £10.72 per Club membership)

❑ I enclose a cheque or postal order payable to Egmont World Limited.

❑ Please charge my MasterCard / Visa account.

Card number: | | | | | | | | | | | | | | | |

Expiry Date: ____/____ Signature: ______________________

Data Protection Act: If you do **not** wish to receive other family offers from us or companies we recommend, please tick this box ❑. Offer applies to UK only